Thankful
In Every Season

Written by: Chidimma Carter

Illustrated by: Mariya Rana

For my wonderful sons, Chiekezie, Ekene, and Chiwetelu
May you always have a reason to be thankful.

Many thanks to my husband, Michael, for nurturing my dreams over the years.

Joyfull Books™
www.Joyfullbooks.org
inquiries@joyfullbooks.org

Praise for Thankful (in every season)

"In her latest book, "Thankful", author Chidimma Carter invites us into the practice of gratitude alongside our children. The sweet cadence of her poetry makes way for adults and children alike to enter His presence with thanksgiving, counting the many blessings He has lavished on us. From the gifts of nature to family life and everything in between, Mrs. Carter points to a good Father who is worthy of all our praise. "Thankful" is full of the seeds of truth we ought to sow in our children's hearts and minds: that every good and perfect gift is from above."
-Hallie Polanco, owner and director, The Family Room Brentwood

An important book for today's child. This book gloriously depicts the blessings that gratitude brings. Chidimma captures the essence of being thankful in every season.
-Chichi Morris, Column Writer and mother.

Joining a heart of gratitude with simplicity and prose, "Thankful in Every Season" allows young readers to understand how all the intricate blessings create a bouquet of living a life to praise and bring glory to God. Each line of thankfulness is met with uplifting affirmations that young readers can be nourished by, something that is quenching our youth today. With such a timely message, this children's book will not only speak to the heart of a child but also to us as parents, teachers, and leaders in our community to build a strong faith and trust that the Lord is continuing to provide and we are cared for deeply through His miraculous blessing."
- Bianca Mayorga, The Sifted Mama

May we always find a reason to be thankful in every season. May we never forget that for every disappointment there is a blessing. May we always look long enough to find the silver lining and stay in the race long enough to obtain the crown.

Chidimma Carter

I'm thankful for my mom and dad,
For all their love and care.

I'm thankful for my siblings too,
For all the fun times we share.

I'm thankful for my family,
Our peace and joy is so sweet.

I'm thankful for a bed to sleep in,
And for all the yummy food we eat.

I'm so grateful for my clothes and shoes,
For all my books as well.

I'm thankful for all my toys,
There's so much more than I can tell.

I'm thankful for my Street,
And I'm thankful for my state.

I'm thankful for my neighbors too,
My friends are really great.

I'm thankful for the green green grass,
For all the color it brings.

I'm grateful for the trees and sky,
And for all the birds that sing.

I'm thankful for the stories I know,
For all the books I've read.

I'm thankful for my alphabet,
I can say them from my head.

I'm thankful for the stars at night,
For the moon up in the sky.

I'm thankful for the sun so bright,
But glad that it is up so high.

I'm thankful for my dear
grandparents,
For my aunts and uncles too.

So grateful for all my cousins,
And for all the kind things they do.

I'm thankful that I am strong and
bold,
And that I'm polite and kind.

So thankful that I'm loving too,
And that I have a sound mind.

I'm thankful that I'm intelligent,
I can quickly understand.

I'm thankful that I'm hardworking,
And that God has blessed my
hands.

I'm thankful for my school,
And for all my teachers too.

I'm thankful for my church family,
And for all my pastors do.

I'm thankful for the peace I have,
Way deep down in my heart.

I'm grateful for the joy I feel,
From Jesus, I'll never part.

I'm thankful that when I sleep,
I wake up the next day.

And when I'm worried or I am scared,
I know that I can pray.

Of all the things I'm thankful for,
There is just one thing more.

This book itself is not enough,
To tell all I'm grateful for.

So, I'm grateful to The Lord,
For always giving me a reason.

To be thankful and so joyful,
In each and every season.

The Lord's Wonderful Love
By David

"With all my heart I praise the Lord,
and with all that I am, I praise his holy
name!
With all my heart I praise the Lord!
I will never forget how kind he has been."
Psalms 103: 1-2 CEV

More from Joyfull Books™

Ike, Ike & Ike - Learn To Share
Ike, Ike & Ike - Learn To Share (Igbo translation)
Ike, Ike & Ike - Learn To Share (Yoruba translation)

We would like to hear from you, send us an email at
Feedback@Joyfullbooks.org

35102298R00023